For Jane O'Connor,
who trusted me with her characters,
and with thanks to Judy, Lara, and Wendy
—M.L.

For Darryl, with love
—L.S.L.

Copyright © 1995 by Girl Scouts of the United States of America. All rights reserved. Published by Grosset & Dunlap, Inc., a member of The Putnam & Grosset Group, New York, in cooperation with Girl Scouts of the United States of America. GROSSET & DUNLAP is a trademark of Grosset & Dunlap, Inc. Published simultaneously in Canada. Printed in the U.S.A.

Library of Congress Cataloging-in-Publication Data

Leonard, Marcia.
    Marsha's unbearable day / by Marcia Leonard ; illustrated by Laurie Struck Long.
        p.   cm. — (Here come the Brownies ; 10)
    Summary: When Marsha misplaces the teddy bear that has been sent to her Brownie troop by a troop in Australia, she frantically retraces her steps trying to find it.
    [1. Girl Scouts—Fiction.   2. Lost and found possessions—Fiction.
3. Teddy bears—Fiction.]   I. Long, Laurie Struck, ill.   II. Title.   III. Series.
PZ7.L549Mar   1995
[Fic]—dc20
                                                                        95-2652
                                                                          CIP
                                                                          AC

ISBN 0-448-40843-0   A B C D E F G H I J

HERE COME THE
BROWNIES
A Brownie Girl Scout Book

Marsha's Unbearable Day

By Marcia Leonard
Illustrated by Laurie Struck Long

Grosset & Dunlap • New York
In association with GIRL SCOUTS OF THE U.S.A.

1

"Today's the day!" Marsha told her friends at the Friday Brownie Girl Scout meeting. "Today Matilda is coming home with me—for the whole weekend!"

Jo Ann was passing out animal crackers for snack time. "I had Matilda last weekend," she said. "I took her to my cousin's wedding."

"The day she stayed with me, we went to a dog show," said Sarah.

"I took her to the toy museum," said Amy.

Marsha grinned. "I bet she liked that!"

Krissy A. was looking puzzled. She had been home with the flu for more than a week. And she'd missed the last meeting.

"Who's Matilda?" she asked. "She must be pretty special if you've taken her all those neat places."

"She's special, all right," said Marsha. "She's been all over the world. Indonesia... Egypt... Holland." She turned to her troop leader, Mrs. Quinones. "Where else, Mrs. Q.?"

"Let's see," said Mrs. Q. "Cameroon... India... and Argentina—right before she came here."

"Wow!" Krissy A. looked around the room. "So where's Matilda now? Do I get to meet her? What's she like?"

Amy winked at the other girls. "Well, she's kind of small...."

"But very cute," Lauren put in.

"She has big brown eyes," Sarah added.

"And the softest brown...fur!" Amy finished with a grin.

"Fur?!" Krissy A. looked so surprised, Marsha and the others burst out laughing.

Corrie reached into her backpack. "Here she is!" She held up a little toy koala. "Matilda, meet Krissy A. Krissy, this is Waltzing Matilda." She made the koala do a little bow.

"Oh, you guys!" Krissy said with a laugh. "I thought you were talking about a real person. You know, a Girl Scout. Like us!"

"Matilda *is* a Girl Scout—I mean, a Girl Guide. That's what they're called in Australia," said Corrie. "See her smock and her little badge? That's her uniform. It shows she's a Gumnut."

"A what?" asked Krissy A.

"There's a tree that grows in Australia called a gum tree," Mrs. Q. explained. "And the seed pods that grow on that tree are called gumnuts. That's what the youngest Girl Guides are named after. And that's what you see on Matilda's badge."

"So how did Matilda get here?" Krissy A. asked. "Don't tell me she's really been all over the world by herself!"

"She has!" said Marsha. "No fooling."

"She went from troop to troop," Lauren explained. "First the Gumnuts sent her to some Brownies in Indonesia. Then that troop sent her to Holland. And so on and so on until she finally came to us."

"Where is she going next?" asked Krissy A.

"Back to Australia," said Mrs. Q. "Her six-month trip is just about finished."

Krissy A. picked up Matilda. The koala's smock had "Waltzing Matilda" stitched on it in curly gold letters. And it was covered with Girl Scout pins. One was a World Trefoil pin. The rest were pins from the troops Matilda had visited.

"Cool jewels, Matilda," said Krissy. "But what happened to your paw? It looks like somebody chewed on it."

"A puppy did—in Holland," Sarah said.

"I read about it in Matilda's scrapbook."

"Oh, me too," said Corrie.

She took a fat, well-worn notebook from her backpack. "Everyone Matilda stays with puts something in her book. So when she goes back to Australia, the Gumnuts can read about all the things she's done."

The girls paged through the scrapbook. It was full of neat stuff. Tickets and theater programs. Drawings and poems. Pressed flowers and leaves. And lots of photos.

Some entries were not in English. Some even used different alphabets.

Amy came across one written in Spanish. " '¡Hola, amigas!' " she read. "That means 'Hi, friends!' Right, Corrie? What else does it say?"

"Let's see," said Corrie. "It says, 'My name is Juana, and I live on a cattle ranch in Argentina. I'm an *Alita*'—that means 'Little Wing' in Spanish. 'My *Alita* troop and I took Matilda horseback riding.' "

Jo Ann turned to the back of the book. "Here's what I wrote about my cousin's wedding," she said. "And here's a picture of

Matilda and me with the bride and groom."

Marsha peeked over Jo Ann's shoulder. The photo was really cute! She wondered what *she* could do with Matilda that would be special.

Lauren seemed to read her mind. "So what are you and Matilda doing this weekend?" she asked Marsha.

"We're going to my ballet class Saturday," Marsha said slowly. "But besides that...I can't decide."

"As usual!" Lauren smiled. She always teased Marsha about not making up her mind.

"I've got a suggestion," said Mrs. Q. "If you don't have plans for Sunday, this might be fun." She handed Marsha a bright yellow flyer. "And it's something we all could do together."

Marsha read the flyer out loud:

McCORMACK PARK

TEDDY BEAR PICNIC

FUN! FOOD! GAMES!

PRIZES FOR THE OLDEST, BIGGEST, SMALLEST, MOST CUDDLY, BEST DECORATED, AND MOST UNUSUAL BEARS

SUNDAY, 1:00–4:00

"Perfect!" Marsha said. Then she thought of something. "Wait a second. A koala isn't really a bear. Does that matter?"

"No," said Mrs. Q. "Last year there were koalas *and* pandas—even a bunny or two—along with all the teddies."

"Let's enter Matilda in a contest," said Amy. "She'll win a prize for sure."

"But which one?" said Corrie. "Matilda is small *and* cuddly."

"How about 'best decorated'?" Krissy A. asked.

Marsha took the koala from Lauren. "What do *you* think, Matilda?" she asked. She pretended Matilda was whispering in her ear. Then she nodded. "Matilda says she is a 'most unusual bear.' Definitely."

Everyone had to agree.

2

"Waltzing Matilda, Waltzing Matilda. You'll come a-waltzing, Matilda, with me."

Marsha and Lauren sang in the car on the way home from the Brownie meeting. Marsha's little sister, Rosie, clapped and sang along. But her big brother Terrence rolled his eyes.

"Come on," he said. "That's the ninety-ninth time you've sung that song!"

"Great!" said Marsha. "Let's go for a hundred!"

She and Lauren started singing again. And they didn't stop until they pulled into Marsha's driveway.

"Race you to the tree house!" said Lauren.

They piled out of the car and dashed across Marsha's yard. Lauren was ahead— as usual.

"Wait!" Marsha called after her. "Look out for the mud!"

A heavy rain had left a big puddle right below the tree house. Lauren stopped just in time.

"Yuck!" she said. "What a mess!"

"Here," said Marsha. "Step on this rock. Then you can reach the rope ladder."

The girls climbed up, and Marsha took Matilda out of her backpack.

"This is it!" she said. "Our own private tree house. Girls only. Girls and koalas, I mean."

The tree house was Marsha and Lauren's favorite place to play. Sometimes they pretended it was a high-rise apartment. Sometimes it was a pirate ship or spaceship. Or sometimes it was the tower of a castle.

"What should we play today?" Lauren asked.

For once Marsha knew exactly what she wanted to do.

"Let's pretend Matilda is on a Brownie camp-out," she said. "The tree house can be her tent. And we'll be the troop leaders."

"We need more campers," said Lauren. "I know! Let's get some stuffed animals from your room."

They hurried to the house and came back with two teddies, a pig, and a rabbit. Then they sat their campers in a Brownie ring.

Marsha thought they looked cute. But something was missing. "Our tent looks too empty," she said. "We need more stuff."

"Sleeping bags," said Lauren.

"Cooking pans and dishes," said Marsha.

Back and forth they went, stepping over the mud each time. Then finally everything was in place. Each camper had her own blanket and dishes. And there was a set of toy cooking pans with hot dogs made of clay.

"This is so neat!" said Marsha. "I'm going to take a picture of it for Matilda's scrapbook."

She took some shots with her mom's

19

instant camera. The first one was blurry because she moved. But the next three were perfect.

"One for you. One for me. And one for Matilda," said Marsha.

Then Terrence came into the yard. "Hey, what are you two doing up there?" he called.

"Having a Brownie camp-out," Marsha called back. "The tree house is our tent in the woods."

"Then I'll be a grizzly bear!" said Terrence. He growled and made claws with his hands.

"Quick! Pull up the ladder," said Lauren.

Marsha grabbed for the rope—and bumped against Matilda.

"Look out!" yelled Lauren.

But it was too late. The koala went tumbling out the door.

"She'll hit the puddle!" shrieked Marsha. Marsha put her hands over her eyes. She couldn't bear to watch. But she had to know. She peeked out between two fingers and saw Matilda—lying safely in the clean, dry grass.

Lauren wiped her brow. "Whew! That was a close call!"

She and Marsha hurried down the ladder.

Marsha picked up the little koala and looked her over. She sighed with relief. "It's okay. She's fine!"

"Sorry if I scared you," said Terrence. "I really came to tell you that Lauren's dad called. He's coming to pick her up."

"All right," said Marsha. She was ready to stop playing in the tree house anyway.

What if Matilda fell again? It was probably safer to keep her inside.

After Lauren left, Marsha took Matilda upstairs to her room. She put the koala on her desk. Then she got out the scrapbook and opened it to a fresh page.

Carefully, she taped Matilda's photo in place. Then she started to write.

Today, Matilda had a camp-out in my tree house.

She did not put in the part about Matilda falling. After all, nothing had happened to her.

And nothing *will* happen to her, thought Marsha. Because from now on, I'm going to be extra, extra careful!

3

On Saturday, Marsha and her dad made pancakes for breakfast. Marsha sat Matilda on the windowsill while she ate. Close enough to see. But far away from the sticky maple syrup.

Soon it was time for Marsha to get ready for ballet. Marsha loved to dance. And she loved dance class. Madam was the best teacher ever—even if she was very strict!

Marsha got out her pink dance bag and checked to make sure that her ballet slippers were inside. The bag was so full of stuff, sometimes it was hard to tell!

Then she got out her dance clothes.

"What do you think, Matilda?" she said. "Should I wear my pink leotard with the matching leg warmers? Or my red leotard with the flouncy skirt?"

Pink or red. Red or pink. It was so hard to choose.

"Hurry up, Marsha!" her mom called from downstairs. "Hurry or you will be late."

"Coming!" Marsha called back. She quickly put on the pink outfit. Then she saw herself in the mirror.

Oops! There was a streak of dirt across the seat of her leotard. Madam would not approve of that!

Quickly Marsha changed into the red leotard. She grabbed her dance bag with one hand and Matilda with the other. Then she rushed out to the car.

She was one of the last to arrive at the dance studio. But at least the class hadn't started yet!

Marsha changed into her ballet slippers in

the dressing room. Then she put her sneakers and dance bag down by all the others.

"Come on, Matilda," said Marsha. "I can't wait for you to see me dance."

She carried the koala down the hall to the practice room.

Madam was standing outside the door, waiting for latecomers. She stopped Marsha.

"What is this?" she asked, pointing to Matilda. "You know the rule."

Uh-oh. Marsha had forgotten. No toys in class. She felt her face grow hot.

"But Matilda's different," she said. "She's—"

"No toys," Madam said firmly. "Put the koala away, Marsha. Hurry, hurry, hurry."

Marsha hurried. She dashed down the hall and tucked Matilda into her pink dance bag. Then she dashed back to the practice room—just as Madam began the warm-up exercises.

Marsha found a spot at the ballet barre. But her mind was not on ballet.

If only I'd gotten to class early, she thought. Then I could have talked to Madam and explained about Matilda.

"Concentrate, Marsha!" said Madam. "Think, think, think!"

Little by little, Marsha put Matilda out of her mind. At the end of class, Madam almost smiled at her.

"Better, Marsha," she said.

From Madam, that was a big compliment! Marsha practically floated down the hall to the dressing room.

Her mother was waiting for her. "You'll have to hurry, honey," she said. "I need to stop at the post office and the gas station on the way home."

Hurry, hurry, hurry, thought Marsha. It's been hurry, hurry, hurry all morning!

She took off her ballet slippers and handed them to her mom.

"Here, Mom," she said. "Would you put these in my bag?"

Her mother dropped them in. Marsha put

on her shoes. And they rushed out the door.

It was almost 11:30 by the time they got home. Marsha went up to her room and changed. She was sorry Matilda had missed ballet. She would have to make it up to her.

Marsha reached into her dance bag.

That's funny, she thought. Matilda should be right on top!

She dug through her stuff. Once. Twice. Still no koala.

Finally she emptied the bag on her bed.

Out fell her ballet slippers. A towel. A comb and brush. Three hair ribbons and a scrunchie. Four good-luck cards from her Nutcracker show. A dance program. A box of Band-Aids. And an extra pair of tights. But no Matilda.

She was gone!

4

"Mom! Mom!" Marsha raced downstairs to the kitchen. "Matilda's missing. I had her in my dance bag. But now she's gone."

Marsha's mother was making lunch. "Are you sure?" she asked. "Look again. That bag was so full, I couldn't zip it shut."

"I know. But I emptied it all out," said Marsha.

Then she had a terrible thought. "Mom, what if Matilda fell out somewhere?"

"Then she's probably in the house or the

car," said her mom. "Let's take a look."

They hunted everywhere. But there was no sign of Matilda.

"Maybe she fell out at the dance studio," said Marsha. "Can we go back? I've got to find her!"

Marsha's father took over making lunch. And her mom drove her back to the studio.

Madam was still there. But Matilda was not.

Marsha sat down on a bench in the dressing room. Her shoulders slumped. And all at once she started to cry.

"Oh, honey! We'll find her!" Marsha's mom gave her a hug. "Let's go over this again. When was the last time you saw Matilda?"

Marsha wiped her eyes on her sleeve. "When I brought her back here. After

Madam told me I couldn't take her into class."

Marsha got up from the bench. She pretended to carry Matilda into the room.

"Then what?" said her mother.

Marsha walked over to the first bench and bent down. "Then I tucked her into my pink bag. Right here."

Marsha's mom looked puzzled. "I thought your bag was under there." She pointed to the second bench.

Marsha eyes got wide. She smacked her forehead. "Oh, no! I put Matilda in the wrong bag! How could I be so dumb?"

"You were in a hurry," said her mother. "That's when mistakes can happen."

Marsha nodded miserably. "Matilda must have gone home with someone else.

But who? There were a zillion pink dance bags in here."

Marsha tried to remember the kids in her class. Allison...Janey...Taylor....There were so many! She didn't even know them all.

Marsha's mom got a class list from Madam. And right after lunch, Marsha started calling.

First she tried the kids she knew pretty well. None of them had seen Matilda.

Then she called the next girl on the list—Belinda Cruz. Marsha remembered Belinda. She had very short hair and very big glasses. And she was a third grader at another school.

Belinda's father answered the phone.

"Belinda's at karate class," he said. "Would you like to leave a message?"

Marsha took a deep breath. She told Mr. Cruz about Matilda and the dance bag mix-up.

"Well, you called the right place," said Mr. Cruz. "Belinda *did* find a koala in her dance bag."

"She did?!" Marsha was almost yelling. "Can I come over and get her? Right now?"

"Sure," said Mr. Cruz.

By the time Marsha's mom drove her to the Cruzes' house, Belinda was home.

"Oh, was that *your* koala?" she said. "My big sister packed my dance bag after class. So I didn't find it till I got home. Then, boy, was I surprised!"

Marsha grinned. "I'm sorry about the

mix-up. But I'm glad Matilda is okay." She looked around. "Where is she?"

Belinda stared at the toes of her sneakers. "We-ell," she said slowly, "she's not here."

Marsha's jaw dropped. "What do you mean?"

"Don't worry. Matilda's fine," Belinda said in a rush. "See, I figured she belonged to a Girl Scout—because of all her pins. So I took her over to my neighbor Emily Randall. Emily's a Brownie. I thought she could take Matilda to school on Monday and find out who she belonged to."

She looked at Marsha. "I'm sorry," she said. "It seemed like a good idea."

Marsha swallowed hard. "Where does Emily live?" she asked. "Can you take me to her house?"

"Sure," said Belinda. "It's just down the street."

"Good," said Marsha.

She wanted to believe Matilda was okay. But she knew she wouldn't be happy until the koala was in her arms again.

5

It was a short walk to Emily's house. Belinda rang the bell. A plump woman with a friendly smile answered it. She had on a pretty blue-and-green patchwork vest. A toddler clung to her matching blue skirt.

"Hi, Mrs. Randall," said Belinda. She introduced Marsha and Marsha's mom. Then she explained why they were there.

"Come on in," said Mrs. Randall. "Emily's at the park with her sisters and brother. But the koala is here."

They trooped inside.

Marsha tried not to stare. The Randalls'
house was full of shelves. And the shelves
were full of stuff. Rolls of bright cloth.
Toys and games and tons of stuffed animals.
Little statues and other things that looked as
if they'd come from far-off places.

Mrs. Randall could tell Marsha was
surprised.

"Looks kind of like a department store, doesn't it?" she said. "But with five kids, a mother who makes quilts, and a father who's a travel agent—well, things pile up."

She smiled at Marsha. "Now, let's find your koala."

"She was on the coffee table when I left," Belinda said helpfully.

Marsha looked at the table. She did not see Matilda.

"She *was* on the coffee table," said Mrs. Randall. "But then David found her. Didn't you, lovie?" She gave the toddler a pat. "He tried to feed her his graham cracker. And I'm afraid it was kind of mushy."

Marsha's stomach did a flip. She pictured Matilda's soft fur covered with cracker mush.

"Don't worry," said Mrs. Randall. "I

cleaned her face and outfit with a damp cloth. They're both as good as new."

She disappeared into the bathroom and came back with Matilda's smock.

Marsha looked at it closely. The smock was a little damp. But it was clean. The pins looked okay, too.

"I put her up high, out of David's reach," said Mrs. Randall.

She led them to a shelf full of toys. Then she frowned.

"Hmmm. I could have sworn I put her here. Guess I was wrong. Anyway, she's somewhere in the house. We'll just have to look."

Marsha's stomach did a double flip. Finding something in this house was not going to be easy!

First they searched the toy shelves. They turned up lots of teddy bears. Even two koalas. But no Matilda.

Then they searched the rest of the shelves. Any other day, Marsha would have liked looking at the carved wooden masks, the silk fans, and the other cool stuff Mr. Randall had brought back from his travels. But now all she could think of was Matilda.

"I wonder...," Mrs. Randall said at last. "My son Paul had some friends over earlier today. They played animal hospital. Maybe they did something with your koala."

Marsha imagined four boys covering Matilda with sticky Band-Aids. Maybe even cutting her open for a pretend operation.

"Oh, no!" she exclaimed.

"I'm sure Matilda is fine," Mrs. Randall said quickly. "One of the kids probably knows where she is. I'll ask them when they get home. I'll give you a call as soon as we find her."

"Thanks," Marsha said sadly.

She really wanted to keep looking. But it was clear that Mrs. Randall thought the search was over—at least for now.

"My husband and I are going out to dinner tonight. But I'll call you before we leave," Mrs. Randall told Marsha. "In the meantime, don't worry."

"I'll try not to," said Marsha.

But when she got home, Marsha *did* worry. Tomorrow was the Teddy Bear

Picnic. What if the Randalls didn't find Matilda in time? What if Matilda wasn't even there?

Without her smock and notebook, she'd look like just another stuffed animal. No one who found her would ever guess how special she was.

Oh, Matilda! Where are you? thought Marsha.

The afternoon wore on, and there was no call from Mrs. Randall.

Finally, just before dinner, the phone rang.

Marsha ran to answer it. "Hello?" she said hopefully.

It was Mrs. Randall. "I'm really sorry," she said. "The kids and I looked all over. But we still can't find Matilda."

Marsha's heart sank.

"I don't know what else to tell you," Mrs. Randall went on. "I have to meet my husband at the restaurant now, but tomorrow we'll search the house from top to bottom. I'll call you if we have any luck. Okay?"

Marsha's throat was so tight she could hardly speak. "Okay, Mrs. Randall. 'Bye."

She hung up the phone. Now what am I going to do? she thought.

The phone rang again. This time it was Lauren.

"Hi, Marsha," she said. "How's Matilda?"

Marsha was quiet. How could she tell Lauren that Matilda was lost? Then again, Lauren was her best friend. They told each other everything.

Marsha took a deep breath. And she poured out the whole story.

"Wow!" said Lauren. "Do you want me to come over?"

"Oh, Lauren, that would be great," said Marsha. "Let's ask our parents if you can sleep over. Then you can help me figure out what to do."

By the time Marsha hung up the phone, she was feeling a little better. If anyone could help her out of this mess, it was Lauren.

6

"This is the worst day of my whole life!" Marsha told Lauren later that night. "Matilda's been all over the world, without any problems. Then she visits me and—poof!—she disappears. What am I going to tell the troop? What will I tell the Gumnuts?" Marsha groaned and flopped down on her bed.

"Hey, don't give up yet!" said Lauren. "The picnic isn't till one o'clock tomorrow."

"Maybe I could pretend I'm sick," said Marsha. "Then I wouldn't have to go."

"Yeah, but you'd still have to send Matilda," said Lauren. "Now if you said that *she* was sick..."

Marsha giggled.

"Good, you can still laugh," said Lauren. "Come on. Let's figure out what to do."

Marsha thought for a moment. "My neighbor put up posters when she lost her cat," she said. "Maybe we could do that for Matilda."

"Yeah!" said Lauren. "We could use the pictures you took in the tree house."

Marsha sighed. "The only thing is, I still have to go to the picnic tomorrow—without Matilda."

Then suddenly she had an idea. "What if we buy another koala and take it instead?

I don't mean to *fool* anyone. We'll tell
Mrs. Q. and the troop what happened."

"I get it," said Lauren. "The new koala
would just take Matilda's place until we
find her, right?"

"Right," said Marsha. "*If* we find her."

"Don't worry," said Lauren. "We will."

Marsha was glad Lauren had come over.
Good friends always made big problems
seem smaller.

It was late, so the girls went to bed. But
Marsha couldn't sleep. She felt as if she'd
been on a roller coaster all day. Up and
down. Up and down. Thinking she'd found
Matilda. Then finding out Matilda was still
lost.

What a lot of trouble from one dumb
mistake, thought Marsha. From now on,

I've got to be more careful. Especially when I'm in a hurry! And especially with other people's stuff!

*   *   *

The next morning, the girls got started on their posters. Then just before noon, Marsha put Matilda's smock and notebook in her backpack. And her dad walked her and Lauren to the toy store downtown.

They were passing a place called The Travel Center when Marsha suddenly stopped.

Ooof! Lauren bumped into her. "Hey, what's the idea? Why did you stop?"

"Look! Look there!" Marsha pointed.

In the window of The Travel Center was a banner that read, VISIT AUSTRALIA, THE LAND DOWN UNDER.

Below it was a little scene: three stuffed
animals having a picnic on the beach.
One was a kangaroo. One was a platypus.
And one was a koala.

"It's Matilda!" shouted Marsha.

"Are you sure?" asked her dad.

"Positive!" said Marsha. "I can tell by
her paw. The one the puppy nibbled on."

"It *is* Matilda," cried Lauren. "We found
her!"

Marsha suddenly felt light—as if a hundred-pound pack had been lifted from her back.

"But how did she get here?" asked Lauren.

"That's what I'd like to know!" said Marsha.

She tried the door of The Travel Center. It was locked. Then she noticed some words painted on the glass.

"Hey! Look at this! It says, 'Jack Randall, Owner.' Mrs. Randall said her husband was a travel agent. Maybe he put Matilda in the window."

"I bet you're right," said Marsha's dad. "Now the question is, how do we get her out in time for the picnic? It looks like this place is closed."

"Let's call the Randalls," said Marsha. "We can ask Mr. Randall to come and open the door."

She peered into the window. "Don't worry, Matilda. We'll get you out of there."

"Excuse me," said a voice behind Marsha.

She turned and saw a tall, slim man. He had a toy koala in one hand and a set of keys in the other. It had to be . . .

"Mr. Randall?"

"Yes?" said the man.

"I'm Marsha," she said. "I was at your house yesterday, looking for a toy koala."

"The one in the window." Mr. Randall nodded. "I'm sorry, Marsha! I saw it yesterday when I came home for lunch. I thought it would be perfect for my Australia display. So I brought it back here. I thought it belonged to one of my kids," he explained. "They let me use their toys sometimes."

Then Mr. Randall unlocked the door. In a moment Matilda was in Marsha's arms.

She gave the koala a big hug. "Oh, Matilda. Am I glad to see you!"

"I wish I'd known you were looking for her yesterday," said Mr. Randall. "But no one thought to ask me until now. I came straight here to make the switch."

Marsha smiled. "It's okay. Matilda's back, safe and sound. That's all that matters."

7

Marsha was so happy. She and Lauren skipped all the way to McCormack Park. But she kept a tight hold on Matilda!

The park was crowded. Every kid seemed to be carrying a bear or a bunny, a panda or a pig.

Finally Marsha spotted Mrs. Q. and her Brownie Girl Scout troop.

"Hi!" she called.

"Hi, you guys!" said Corrie. "Hi, Matilda. Are you ready for the picnic?"

"She sure is," said Lauren.

"All right!" said Amy.

Jo Ann turned to Marsha. "What did you and Matilda end up doing yesterday?" she asked.

Marsha rolled her eyes. "It's a long story. I'll tell you later."

"Come on," said Lauren. "Let's take Matilda over to the judging tables."

Marsha checked out the other stuffed animals in the "most unusual" group. One was a panda dressed in a pretty Chinese costume. Another was a windup bear that growled. One blew real bubbles from a bubble pipe.

Nice, thought Marsha. But nowhere near as special as Matilda!

"Just set your koala right here on the table," the judge told her.

Marsha put down Matilda's notebook. But suddenly she didn't want to let go of Matilda. Not after all she'd been through to find her!

"Don't worry. I'll take good care of her. Girl Scout's Honor," said the judge. She smiled at Marsha. "I was a Brownie once, too. So I know what that means."

Marsha sighed with relief. "Thanks," she said. "Thanks a lot!" And she put Matilda on the table.

"Let's go play some games," said Amy.

"Okay," said Krissy S. "What should we do first? Water balloon toss? Three-legged race? Face painting?"

"Don't ask Marsha," teased Lauren. "The picnic will be over before she decides."

Marsha stuck her tongue out at Lauren.

MOST UNUSUAL
BEARS

"Just for that, you have to be my partner in the water balloon toss. And if you aren't nice to me, you are going to get wet!"

Lauren held up her hands. "Wait. I take it all back. I'm not ready for a bath."

She and Marsha lined up for the game. But it was Marsha who got wet. She missed a catch, and the balloon splattered at her feet.

"Ooooh! Sorry," said Lauren.

"No big deal," said Marsha. She was much too happy to let soggy sneakers bother her.

Next they played the ring toss game.

Then they ran the three-legged race.

"Whew, am I hot!" said Marsha. "Let's take a break."

Mrs. Q. bought popsicles for the whole troop. Marsha had orange. Lauren had cherry.

When everyone finished, Mrs. Q. checked her watch. "The judge will be announcing the contest winners soon," she said. "Should we head over to the tables?"

"Yeah, let's go!" said Amy. "I want a front-row seat."

The girls sat together on the grass. They clapped as the judge handed out ribbons for the oldest, the biggest, the smallest, the most cuddly, and the best decorated bears.

Then it was time for the most unusual bear.

The judge held up a big blue ribbon.

Marsha grabbed Lauren's hand for good luck.

"And the winner is...Waltzing Matilda, a koala from Australia!"

The Brownies clapped and cheered. Marsha loudest of all.

"Waltzing Matilda is truly unusual," the judge went on. "In just six months she has traveled farther than most of us will in a lifetime. And the amazing thing is, she has never gotten lost!"

Marsha and Lauren looked at each other. "At least not for long!" Lauren whispered.

Marsha smiled. Tonight she would add the story of Matilda's final adventure to the scrapbook. Then she would fasten Matilda's ribbon to the very last page. A blue ribbon for Waltzing Matilda. A most unusual bear.

Girl Scout Ways

Your class or Brownie Girl Scout troop can sponsor a traveling teddy bear, too—just like the Australian Gumnuts did. All you need is a teddy and a sturdy notebook.

- Write a short note in the front of the notebook to explain to your teddy's future hosts what you are doing—just like this note that went with Matilda:

> Hi! My name is Matilda and I come from Sydney, Australia. Gumnut Troop 241 has sent me off to see the world. Won't you please help by writing in my journal so my Gumnut friends can read about everyone I meet and everything I see and do?

Don't forget to include your name, address, and the date you want your teddy to come home.

- Start small by mailing your teddy to a local Girl Scout troop or to nearby friends. If you know someone who lives farther away, you may want to send the teddy to them, too.

- When your teddy comes home, don't forget to write back to everyone who helped it out along the way. Who knows—you might make some new friends, too!